DOG TALES

by Janet McLean   illustrated by Andrew McLean

TICKNOR & FIELDS BOOKS FOR YOUNG READERS / New York 1995

To Donny, Psyche, Charles, Maggie, and Kipper, our dogs.

Library of Congress Cataloging-in-Publication Data: McLean, Janet.   Dog Tales / by Janet McLean ; illustrated by Andrew McLean. —1st American ed.   p. cm.   Summary: A lively, rhyming account of all the various activities that make up a dog's life.   ISBN: 0-395-72288-8   [1. Dogs—Fiction. 2. Stories in rhyme.] I. McLean, Andrew, ill. II. Title.   PZ8.3.M45987Do 1995   [E]—dc20   94-32221   CIP   AC

Awake

Here are the dogs,
tall, middling, and small . . .

Good morning Groats,

Josh,

Hamish,

they used to be puppies

Heather,

and Peg.

sick dog, hot nose!

Noses

Here are the dogs,
meeting and greeting . . .

sniffing sore knees
and cats up in trees,

quack!

snuffling a bug,
exploring a mug.

Mmm! Smells good, Josh!

Sniff, sniff! What's up there, Hamish?

Ears and Tails

Here are the dogs,
curious and clumsy . . .

on the alert,
and slopping in dirt,

hearing distant thunder rumble,

leave her alone, Heather!

quack!

making precious vases tumble,

sweeping the floor,
and caught in the door.

Ow-ooo!

Chase the mouse, Hamish!

Paws and Jaws

Here are the dogs,
scrabbling around . . .

digging big holes,
scratching at fleas,

how do you do?

Snap! Snap!
Ow-ooch!

gnawing old bones,
snapping at bees.

No, Josh! Drop it!

Playing

Here are the dogs,
outside and in . . .

catching a ball,
riding for a fall,

fetching a stick,

Poor Peg, nursing
a bee sting.

pretending to be sick.

Fighting

Here are two dogs,
snapping and snarling . . .

Stay away, Josh.

Friendly

Here are the dogs,
full of beans . . .

leaping and dancing,
tumbling and prancing.

 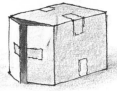

Here are the dogs, quiet and quarrelsome . . .

snuggled up tight,

kept awake all night,

scratched by a claw,

sharing food on the floor,

and showing exactly who's boss.

oh no!

Dirty and Smelly

Here are the dogs,
mucking about . . .

puddling in mud,
all slippery and slushy,

pooh!

Good boy! You got the mouse, Hamish!

rolling in rubbish,
all stinky and mushy.

Catch that dirty dog!

Running Away

Here is the dirty dog,
not wanting a bath . . .

bounding upstairs,
over beds, over chairs,

helter-skeltering around,
then scampering down.

room for me?

Squeaky Clean

Here are the dogs,
wet and bedraggled . . .

shivering, shaking,

wondering why,

no room!

duck-diving dog

hosed-down, and dry.

bad dog!

Scared

Here are the dogs,
quivering and shivering . . .

worried by cats
and machines that are frightening,

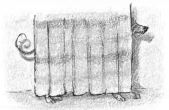

quack !

scratching the door
to escape from the lightning.

Come in, Heather.

playing dead

Clever

Here are the dogs,
pleased as can be . . .

climbing up a ladder,

walking on a wall,

bringing home the shopping,
standing up tall,

walk time

fetching the paper,

collecting an egg,

opening the letters,

learning to beg.

Naughty

Here are the dogs,
cunning and crafty . . .

lying in wait for a man at the gate,

doggedly stalking a duck,

chewing the washing,

wrestling a cushion,

chasing a big red truck.

Noisy

Here are the dogs,
yapping and yodeling . . .

singing a tune,

serenading the moon.

Asleep

sweet dreams

Here are the dogs, small, middling, and tall . . .

Goodnight, sleep tight, Groats, Hamish, Josh, Heather, and Peg.